3 4028 07781 7980
HARRIS COUNTY PUBLIC LIBRARY

J 398.209
Mandell,
A donkey reads
from a Turkish folktale
WITHDRAWN
$16.95
ocn542263523
11/22/2011

For Aviva

Text copyright © 2011 Muriel Mandell.
Illustrations copyright © 2011 André Letria. All rights reserved. No part of this book may be reproduced or transmitted in any form or by any means, electronic or mechanical, photocopying, recording, or by any information storage and retrieval systems that are available now or in the future, without permission in writing from the copyright holder and the publisher.

Published in the United States of America by Star Bright Books, Inc., 30-19 48th Avenue, Long Island City, NY 11101.

The name Star Bright Books and the Star Bright Books logo are registered trademarks of Star Bright Books, Inc. Please visit www.starbrightbooks.com. For bulk orders, email: orders@starbrightbooks.com.

Hardback ISBN-13: 978-1-59572-255-3
Paperback ISBN-13: 978-1-59572-256-0

Star Bright Books / NY / 00103100
Printed in China (WKT) 9 8 7 6 5 4 3 2 1
Printed on FSC certified paper.

Library of Congress Cataloging-in-Publication Data

Mandell, Muriel.
 A donkey reads / adapted by Muriel Mandell from a Turkish folktale ; illustrations by André Letria.
    p. cm.
 Summary: In a small village in Anatolia, even the poorest villager is expected to pay tribute to a tyrranical Mongol ruler, but the wiseman, Nasreddin Hoca, finds a way to make an aged donkey seem most valuable.
  ISBN 978-1-59572-255-3 (hardback : alk. paper) -- ISBN 978-1-59572-256-0 (pbk. : alk. paper)
 [1. Turkic peoples--Folklore. 2. Folklore--Turkey. 3. Nasreddin Hoca (Legendary character)] I. Letria, André, ill. II. Title.
 PZ8.1.M29765Don 2011
 398.2094961--dc22
 [E]
                    2010002989

A Donkey Reads

Adapted from a Turkish folktale

By
Muriel Mandell

Art by
André Letria

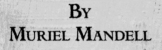

Star Bright Books
New York

Once, many years ago, a small village in Anatolia inhabited by the Seljuks was conquered by the Mongols.

Their leader demanded tribute from even the poorest of the villagers.

Mustafo and his family wondered what they could give. They lived in a tumbled down shack and barely had enough to eat. They owned an old donkey, but he was no longer strong enough to carry even the smallest of the family's many children.

"Husband," said Mustafo's wife, "we can give the donkey. He no longer earns his feed. He may save us from the wrath of the Mongols."

"That donkey has served us well for many years, but he will not do for the greedy tyrant," Mustafo said sadly. "He will surely have me beaten for daring to give such an unworthy gift."

Since his family could spare nothing else, Mustafo agreed to lead the donkey to the tyrant's stable.

One by one the villagers presented their offerings:

a huge bag of grain,

a fat rooster,

a basket of apricots,

a baked baklava,

a baby lamb,

and a plump rabbit.

Mustafo looked at the gifts for the greedy tyrant and thought of his hungry children. He slowly led his aged donkey to the Mongol, and then bowed.

"Sire," said Mustafo, "I beg you to receive my humble gift."

The Mongol stepped down from his dais and strode toward where Mustafo was standing. "You insult me!" the tyrant screamed. "What would you have me do with that pitiful creature? He's a poor excuse for a donkey."

"Sire," said Mustafo, "he is very gentle. Look at his fine intelligent eyes."

The Mongol snorted, "You will pay for this indignity with a beating!"

"But Sire, he *does* have intelligent eyes." So spoke Nasreddin Hoca, the village wise man. "I believe that I can teach him to read."

"You jest! Your jest will cost you this villager's beating!" the tyrant roared.

"I *can* teach him to read—if I want to," Nasreddin said softly.

The tyrant looked at him. "Then do it. I order you to teach him to read. Bring him before me in exactly one month. He will read by then—or else!"

Nasreddin took the reins of the donkey as the Mongol stomped away. Mustafo and the other villagers were very frightened. "How can you teach this ordinary donkey to read?" Mustafo asked him. "Neither my wife, nor my children, nor I can master the scribbles on a page."

"I will begin training the donkey right away," Nasreddin insisted. "You shall see."

For the next month he groomed the donkey until his coat shined and the animal held his head high with pride.

Each morning and each evening Nasreddin fed the donkey in a most unusual way. He put barley between the pages of a book. For many days he turned the pages slowly—very slowly—and let the donkey eat the barley. After a time the impatient donkey began to turn the pages with his tongue in order to get at the feed.

Then, for a few days just before the month was up, Nasreddin offered the donkey no feed.

On the agreed upon day, he took the donkey to the tyrant's stable. "Well," said the Mongol, "my donkey looks much improved, but if you boasted idly . . ."

The tyrant ordered his grooms to put a huge tome—one with many pages—before the donkey.

The hungry animal began to turn the pages with his tongue. He turned page after page after page, more and more quickly. But, of course, there was no barley to be found. The hungry donkey began to bray loudly. He brayed and he brayed and he brayed.

"What is this?" the tyrant asked. "You said you would teach him to read."

Nasreddin looked at the tyrant with a lifted eyebrow. "Why, Sire," he said, "you saw him turn the pages. You saw how quickly he read. He read to the end of that large book, indeed, one he had never seen before. You even heard him read aloud.

"Read aloud?" asked the puzzled Mongol.

"Yes," said Nasreddin, a sly smile crossing his lips, "a donkey does not talk like a man."

And the villagers and the Wise Man laughed and laughed. Perhaps even the Mongol had to smile, though we don't know whether Nasreddin escaped the threatened beating.

Nasreddin Hoca was a thirteenth century teacher, judge, and imam from a village in Anatolia in what is now Turkey. He wrote many stories that have survived more than 700 years. These tales are marked by his offbeat humor even when critical of both those in power and those oppressed during the Mongol rule.

Though little known in the West, Nasreddin and his descendants are honored throughout Turkey and the Middle East.

Harris County Public Library
Houston, Texas